This book belongs to

_____

_____

_____

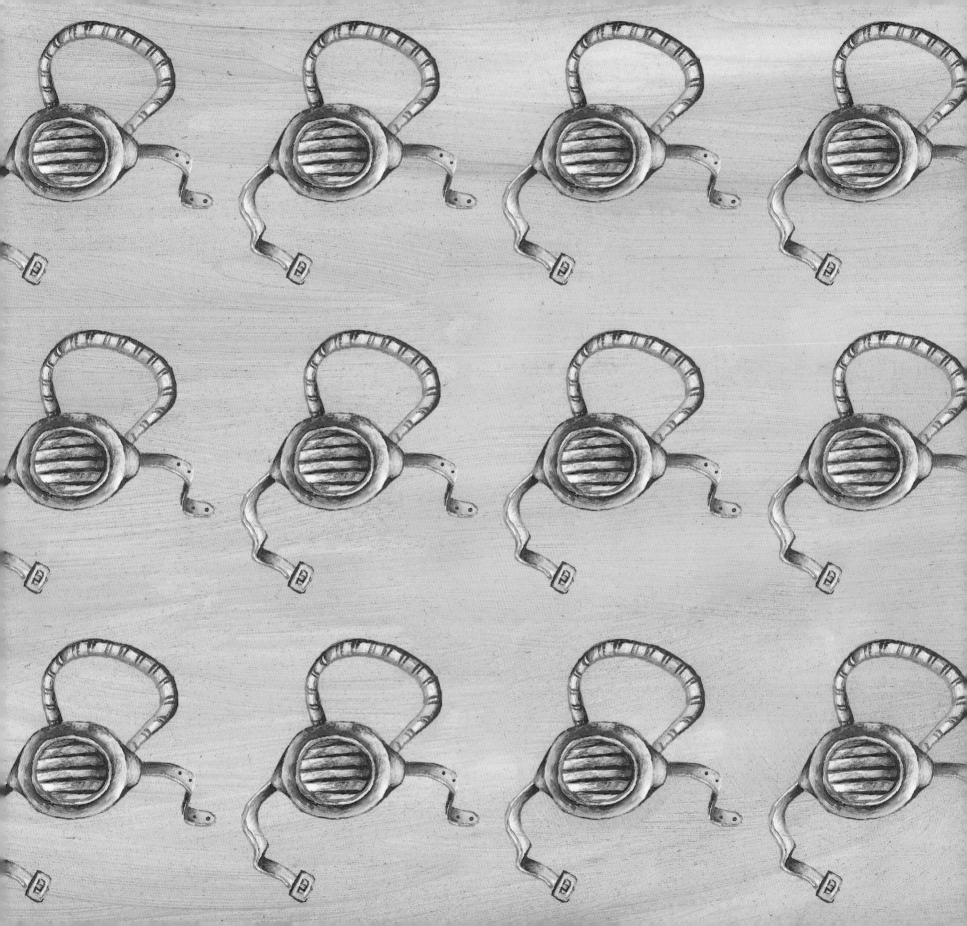

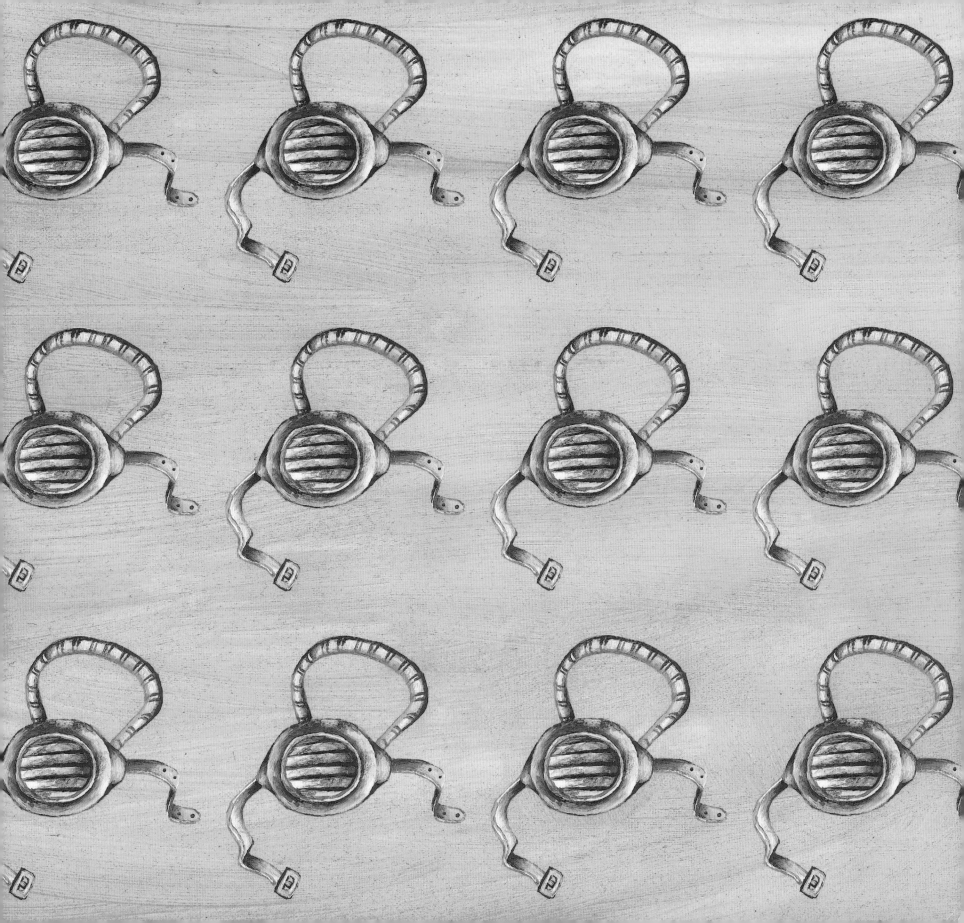

For Alexi, Albert and Angélique – DM
For Lola – TA
For my Mum and Dad – EB

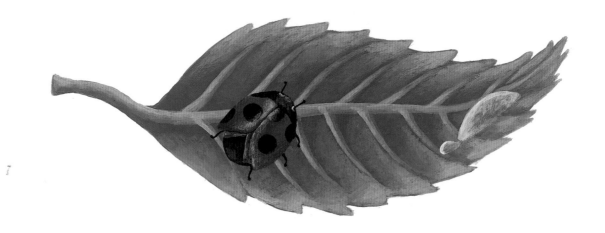

Special thanks to Soma Mitra-Chubb,
Mark Butcher and Alistair Brown

First Published in 2008 by Vanilla Chinchilla Books

24 Ashworth Mansions, Elgin Avenue, London W9 1JP

Text copyright © 2008 Devika Malik & Temi Akinwande

Illustration copyright © 2008 Emma Bray

ISBN 978-0-9556713-0-2 (paperback)

2 4 6 8 10 9 7 5 3 1

A CIP catalogue record for this title is available from the British Library.

Printed and bound in China using PEFC certified paper

The Dirty Imbars

by Devika Malik and Temi Akinwande
illustrated by Emma Bray

Matthew, Meg and Molly
Are not quite what they seem,
Their mission is to save the world,
Working as a team.

They call themselves the Buffins.
And with mystic powers by night,
They transform into heroes,
When nobody's in sight.

They use a crystal ball
To whoosh to far-off lands,
Over hills and mountains high
Across the seas and sands.

By light of day, the Buffins

Are just like you and me,

Fun-loving children

Who are naughty ... occasionally.

They like to mess with water
And chew on sticky sweets.
They drive their parents crazy
And kick the autumn leaves.

After school they meet up
To frolic in the park,
But everything begins to change
When the day grows dark.

The Buffins gaze into their ball,
Held out on Molly's hand.
Colour swirls and misty twirls
Reveal the Imbar land.

The Imbars are a messy bunch
With rubbish piled up high.
This leads to loads of problems,
Which no one can deny.

Roads are blocked with traffic jams
And everyone is late.
Years of neglect and laziness
Have left them in this state.

The beauty of nature is hidden,
Under mounds of grimy dirt.
The Imbars want to tidy up,
But who will get there first?

The smell is so disgusting,
All Imbars wear a mask.
Even for the gifted Buffins
This proves a mighty task.

Zuzu Imbar calls a meeting. "Things have gone too far!"
He pleads with all the citizens to rouse the Buffin stars.

The rats have taken over and are rapidly spreading disease.
But Zuzu thinks the Buffins will tackle them with ease.

He takes the Buffins on a tour
Around the crumbling city.
Once such a majestic place,
Its downfall is such a pity.

The rats sit on rubbish heaps
At every street corner.
Living under decking
And in places where it's warmer.

The rodents, once such shy beasts, have lost their sense of fear,
Leaping on a tray of food the second it appears.

Emerging from the bushes, so cheeky they've become,
Posing for the tourists and basking in the sun.

They never hesitate to steal
Sweets from little babies

Or to nibble at the ankles
Of delicate young ladies.

Matthew tells the Imbars,
"You're responsible for the mess.
If you had kept the city clean,
You wouldn't be so stressed."

Molly says "We can help,
But only on one condition.
You Imbars must change your ways,
And make cleanliness a tradition."

The Imbars promise to change,
And Zuzu gives his word.
So, with no time to waste,
the Buffins' orders are heard.

BOTTLES

Meg tells the Imbars, "Take your rubbish to the dump."
Everybody does their part – even the wise man with his stump.

After school, young children
Take dustpans, mops and brooms.
They sweep the streets until they're clean
And tidy up their rooms!

For once the selfish Imbars start working as a team,
Helping one another to fulfil their special dream.

Plastic bottles, cans and stuff are collected for recycling.
The Imbars hadn't thought of this! it's really quite enlightening.

Animals come from far and wide
To help the Imbars out,

The worthiness of the cause
Leaves them in no doubt.

Snakes clean dirty drainpipes
And hedgehogs brush the gutters.
Elephants carry bin bags
And foxes dust the shutters.

Beside the city's rubbish dump, rat houses are built in hollows.
As predicted by the Buffins, the rats soon start to follow.

The Buffins construct
a conveyor belt,
Connecting the
two sites.

When the vermin run across,
They generate power and light.

The Imbars are delighted
And give the Buffins a cheer.
Zuzu gives them all a hug —
His happiness is all too clear.

The Buffins are given medals
And all are asked to stay.
They thank the Imbars nicely,
But it's time to go away.

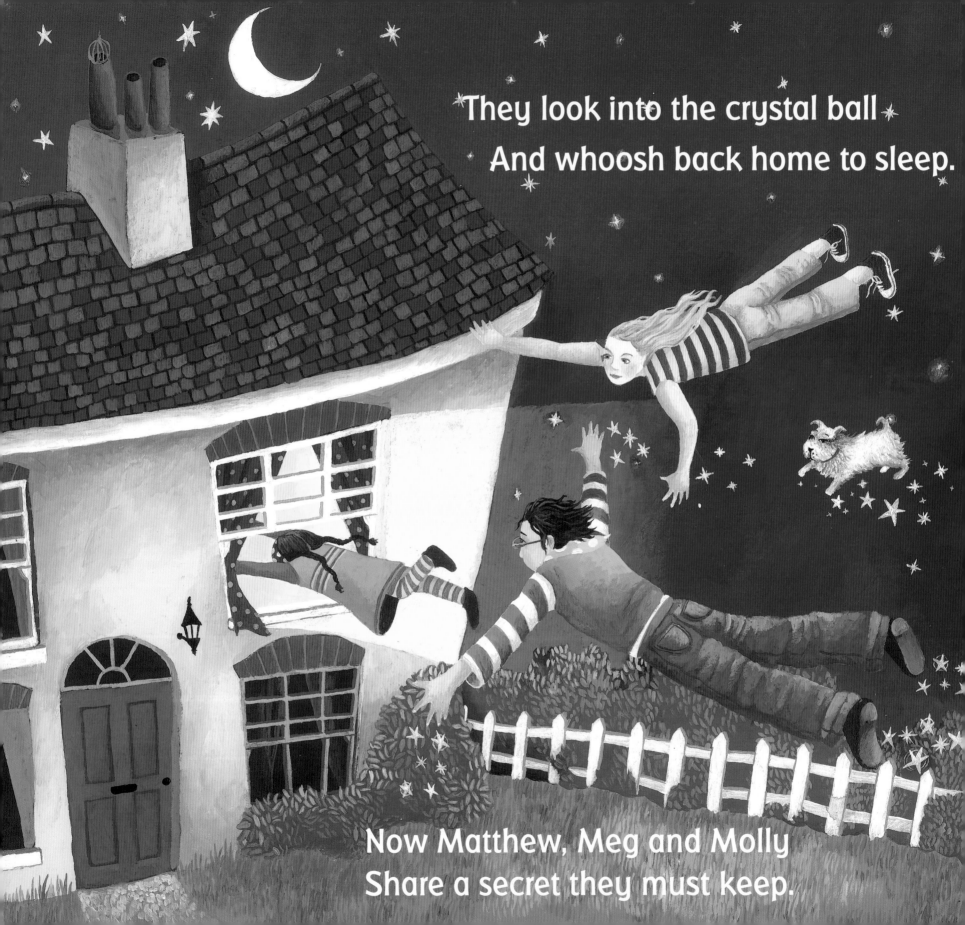

They look into the crystal ball
And whoosh back home to sleep.

Now Matthew, Meg and Molly
Share a secret they must keep.

Molly's mummy wakes her up and asks her if she's rested,

Not knowing that throughout the night

Her powers have been tested!

In our topsy-turvy world

Their work is never done,

So we wait impatiently

For the adventures still to come...

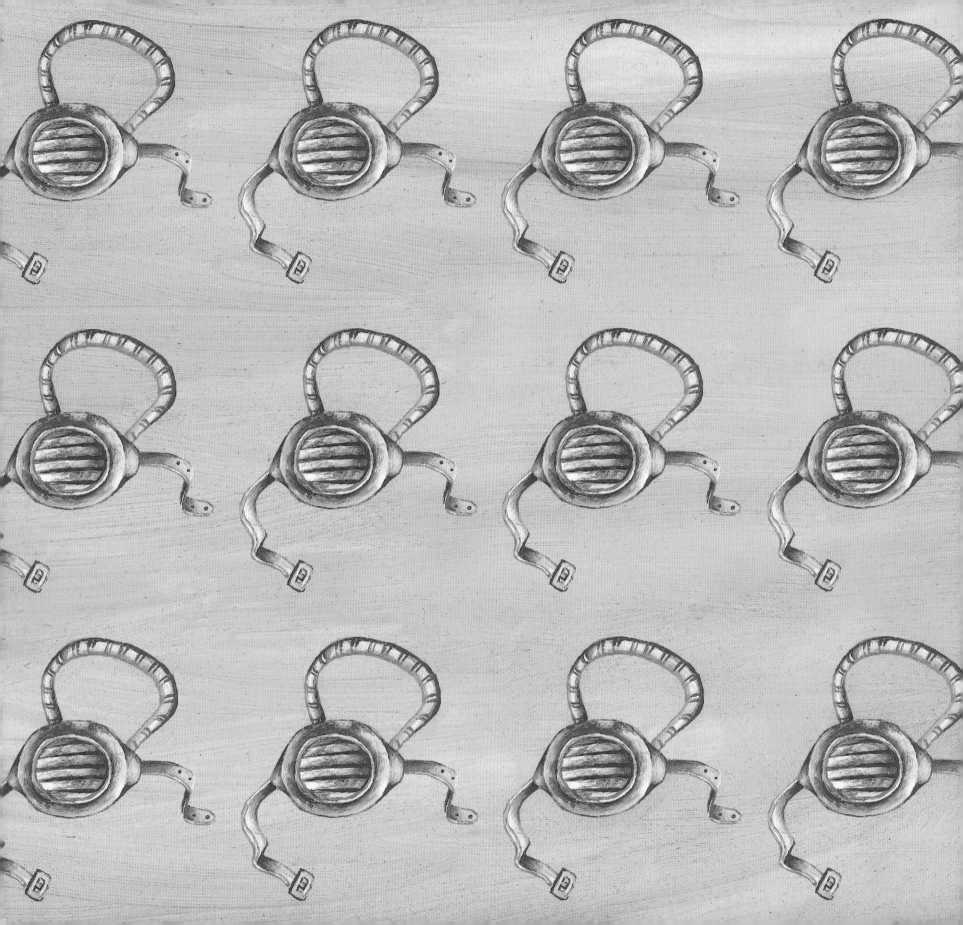

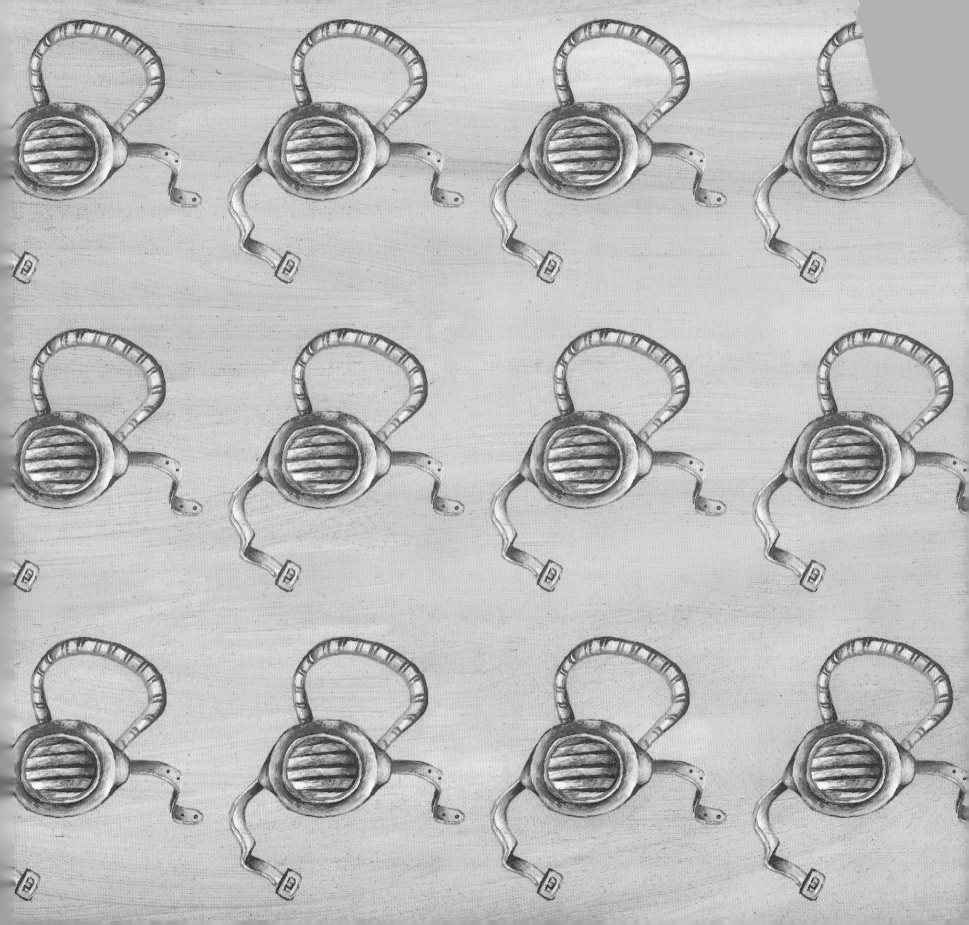

Devika Malik and Temi Akinwande are two mothers who were inspired to write a book that celebrates ethnic diversity and shows children simple ways they can improve the environment.

By purchasing this book, you will be helping children in the developing world gain the lifelong gift of education. Ten per cent of the profits will be donated to Room to Read (www.roomtoread.org), a charity which partners with local communities throughout the developing world to establish schools, libraries and other educational infrastructure.

Room to Read®

The book has been published by Vanilla Chinchilla Books, founded by Devika Malik.